THE WOMAN FROM KLEADITON

A Cosmic Love Story

By

Arijit Kora

DISCLAIMER

The characters, events, and dialogues in this book are entirely fictional. Any resemblance to real persons, living or dead, is coincidental and not intended by the author.

The views expressed by the characters in this work are their own and do not necessarily reflect the views of the author.

This book is a work of fiction, and any references to historical events, real people, or real places are used fictitiously.

While every precaution has been taken in the preparation of this book, the publisher and author assume no responsibility for errors or omissions, or for damages resulting from the use of the information contained herein.

For permissions, please contact:

Arijit Kora

arijit.kora.in@gmail.com

for more information about the author and upcoming releases.

First Edition: June, 2024

TERMS OF USE

By reading this book, you agree to the following terms and conditions:

Copyright Notice: This book is protected by copyright laws. No part of this book may be reproduced, distributed, or transmitted in any form or by any means without the prior written permission of the author or publisher.

Personal Use Only: The content of this book is intended for personal use only. It is not to be used for any commercial purpose without explicit permission.

Non-Transferable License: The license to read this book is non-transferable. You may not share, lend, or otherwise distribute this book to others.

Disclaimer: The characters, events, and places in this book are entirely fictional. Any resemblance to real persons, living or dead, or actual events is purely coincidental.

Opinions of Characters: The views expressed by the characters in this work are their own and do not necessarily reflect the views of the author.

No Guarantees: The author and publisher make no representations or warranties with respect to the accuracy or completeness of the contents of this book and specifically disclaim any implied warranties.

No Liability: The author and publisher shall not be liable for any loss of profit or any other commercial damages resulting from use or performance of this book.

Changes to Terms: The author reserves the right to change these terms at any time. Changes will be effective when posted.

By reading this book, you acknowledge and agree to these terms. If you do not agree to abide by these terms, please do not proceed to read the book.

For inquiries, please contact: Arijit Kora

arijit.kora.in@gmail.com

First Edition: June, 2024

DEDICATION

For

My Parents, Who teach Me.

Sasa, who guides me.

Gupu, Who inspires me.

TABLE OF CONTENTS

CHAPTER 1
The Voice of a Stranger

The scent of chalk fluttered through the air, mingling with dust particles that sparkled in a string of sunshine in dirty yellow. The peeled-off wallpapers reeked of cigarettes, sweat, and boredom, the years and years of teenage delinquency turning the classroom room into a jail cell with its ceiling cracked, once white floors dusty and brownish, blackboard scraped and stained, the desks written over with colorful markers and the atmosphere tense, heavy and thick with impatience.

Standing in front of the class, Jay could feel his own patience slowly sipping out of him drop by drop. Staring into the faces of his students, he couldn't see anything but tedium, distraction, and disinterest. Almost no one was looking or listening to him; some scratching their desks with the tip of their pen, some were scribbling and doodling in their notebooks, some were gossiping in the back rows, tittering and shooting each other mean looks, some even snoozed with their heads buried in their arms over a desk like on a pillow and others messaged on their phones. Their young faces - tired, sleepy, bored - were slouching like melting candles, their eyes heavy with slumber, lashes fluttering. Jay's every word was just flying in their ears and flying out in a second, their heads filled with everything but the topic he talked about, their minds already in their own bedrooms or outside and free of the dull and nagging teacher.

He wanted to sigh but held it in, his lips turning downward from disappointment. If only his students knew how much he didn't want to be there too, even more than them. He was standing in the room he hated the most, imprisoned by the grey walls and curtain-less windows, shackled by the timetable hanging on the door and reminding him of his own misery, trapped in the never-ending cycle of coming here and leaving without doing even a single meaningfully thing. He was tired of talking and never teaching anyone, exhausted of just spewing words that scattered through the air and never reached his students, bored of seeing the same apathetic faces of teens who would rather be anywhere else but in his class. Disrespected, ignored, forgotten. That was how Jay had felt since starting his job in this high school, and he couldn't bear it anymore.

His eyes snapped open, glimpsing at the time on his watch. There was still five minutes left until the end of the class and he felt as if these five minutes were stretching into hours.

Clearing his throat, he walked back to his desk, placing his hands on it, trying to sound demanding and strict.

"So, you will have a test on this subject next week," he said aloud, his tone flat and dry but his voice deep and clear. "Make sure to learn it well."

The only two students who listened, or at least did so sometimes, pricked their ears. One of them raised their hand.

"Which chapters will be included?"

He looked at her. Cloe, a popular and pretty girl, waited for his answer with her chocolate-brown eyes wide and curious, one hand preparing a pen to write Jay's answer down and the other playing with a string of her long dark hair. She had opened her shoulders and crossed her legs, her skirt slipping further up on them. There was something strange on her face - childish and completely innocent for others, but Jay could see something dark and dirty in her expression, in her rounded eyes, O-shaped glossy lips, and expectant gaze.

"It's the chapters we went over many times already," Jay diverted his look elsewhere. "It's starts from chapter 15 and-"

Suddenly someone spoke up and startled, Jay looked up to see who it was. But everyone was quiet, in their own seats, as bored as before.

He was about to ask if someone had a question when suddenly the voice repeated, now louder and more apparent, coming from somewhere so close as if someone spoke right into his ears.

"Who are you?"

The voice vibrated inside him as though it came from somewhere deep in his consciousness. It came like soft waves that washed over his head and spread through his whole body. This strange feeling shook Jay to his core and made him almost gasp and jump in his spot.

"What is your name?"

It was a woman's voice, the unfamiliar voice of a stranger, and Jay realized that it didn't come from around him, but instead, it was in his own head.

He scowled and wiped his forehead, looking down to hide his face - turning red and hot - from the class.

I'm just imagining things. I'm tired and haven't eaten breakfast.He thought, assuring himself.

He had been delirious only a couple of times in his life - once when he had been young and suffered from a very high fever and another when he had gotten too drunk at college. But now, these illusions had been even more real and shocking than anything he'd experienced ever before, and other than sleeplessness and hunger, he didn't have an excuse.

"Mr. Miller?"

Now, he recognized this voice, and he looked up, startled. Cloe and a few other students watched him curiously, seemingly aware of his momentary dissociation.

"Are you okay, Mr. Miller?" Cloe asked with her high-pitched, chirping voice.

"Yeah, sorry," he forced a smile and looked around. "I was saying..."

"Chapters?"

"Yes, Chapters 15 to 21," he said and nodded, trying to keep his composure. "Please, be prepared for the test. I want all of you to give me better results than the last time."

"Okay, Mr. Miller," Cloe's smile quirked up.

The shrill sound of the bell jerked everyone out of their seats, sending the students running out of the classroom.

Jay smiled respectfully when Cloe strode past him, slipping a lollipop into her mouth.

Left alone, with the chaotic noise coming from the school corridors, Jay began sifting through all the papers he had to grade that night, piling books up in stacks and gathering his notebooks. He was so tired he could barely keep his eyes open, but he had many more hours to suffer through.

He was done for the day but not for life - he had to repeat it all over again tomorrow. So, he got up to leave, his eyes lingering on the window.

The sun peeked through white clouds, brightening the schoolyard. It was crammed with students lazing under trees or hiding behind them to smoke or kiss secretly. The fence walling the yard was shabby and so was the school itself, in need of a renovation, the lawn overgrown and the stadium next to it rusty and rundown.

Folding his arms, Jay sighed, the sickening feeling starting to crawl from his stomach to his throat.

How did he end up here, in this tiny and boring town where nothing happened? How was he living here after being raised in New York City, where the bright lights were always on and something new happened every second? He knew exactly how. After graduating college, he hadn't been able to land a job in the city, so he accepted the first one he had found. He had convinced himself that moving to a new place would be fun and exciting, and though it was at the beginning, he soon got tired of it and began to miss his old, young, colorful life.

Through the window, he could see his reflection in the glass. He took a quick look, almost shyly, as if he was checking someone out. His dark blonde hair needed a cut, the bags under his eyes darker blue than his eyes, he had shaven his face but poorly and had left a few cuts on his chin. Despite it all, he still looked handsome, or at least better than average, with his chiseled jaw, clear skin, Greek nose, broad shoulders, and tall, toned body. It was almost impossible to believe that he had been single for years, and it seemed he'd stay this way if he continued his life as it was.

"Enough self-pity for the day," Jay murmured and turned.

But in an instant, the same voice that had startled him in class repeated.

"Who are you?"

He froze to the spot, staring through the space.

"Who are *you*?"

Everything blurred around, the walls caving in before his eyes. The noise was replaced by strange silence that seemed to fall only around Jay. Even his hands began to go numb, his feet turning heavy and stuck to the floor as if his whole being had been put in an ice cube where he couldn't move an inch.

"Hello?" the voice was demanding. "Can you please answer me?"

"Are you in my head?" Jay finally spoke up. The words slipped out of his lips without his control.

"Are *you* in my head?" the voice echoed back.

It was a woman. That was all Jay could tell. And why would his inner voice be a woman? It made no sense!

"I am in your head, and you are in mine," she said.

"But I have no idea who you are!" Jay laughed, on the verge of going crazy. Was this real?

"And I can say the same," the woman seemed serious, "That's why I'm asking for your name."

"I'm Jay," he finally answered after a minute of hesitation.

"Where do you live? How old are you?"

Her voice was soft and almost soothing, like one of those talented singers. But it was stranger, exotic, with an accent Jay didn't know. It was as if he were listening to some tropical bird chirping a harmonious song.

"I'm 28. I'm from New York but now live in Massachusetts," he responded.

"What's that place?" she sounded confused.

"United States? You don't know?" shocked, Jay laughed and realized how ignorant he had sounded. "Sorry."

"I don't know, no," she said and fell quiet for a while. "I have no idea."

"What about you? Where do you live?" Jay asked. Now it was time he asked her questions. How could anyone not know about the United States? Had she been living in a cave?

"My name is Yelga," the voice came rippling like a mountain river. "I'm from Kleanio, Dastario country."

It took a few seconds for her answer to down on Jay. He swallowed.

"Klea--- what?" now he sounded like the dumb one!

"Kleanio," she repeated calmly.

"But I've never heard of that place! And I'm a geography teacher," Jay guffawed. "Are you coming up with some imaginary town?"

"How dare you!" she said, offended, her voice starting to break. "I am not lying."

"Sorry," feeling bad, Jay apologized. "I just... places is what I know the best and I have never heard of your town or country."

"And I never heard of yours."

"But you speak English so well..." Jay pondered. "It must be some misunderstanding.

"English? I am not talking in that!" Yelga protested. "I'm talking in Dawtan, the most prestigious language, with over 452 other languages in Kleaditon."

"I hear it in English, that's so weird!" Jay was stunned.

"And I hear what you say in Dawtan," Yelga seemed as astonished.

"So Strange…."

Jay fell quiet before he said. "Maybe I don't know all the towns that exist on Earth."

"Earth? What's that?" she asked like one of his students.

Now, Jay's confusion was palpable. He couldn't understand this woman in his head. Was she joking, or was his own mind pulling a stunt on him? Was she his imagination, or was she real? Maybe someone else was pranking him?

"Earth, our planet!" he almost screamed from shock, questions beginning to tangle up in his mind, overwhelm him and make him jitter like an overheated machine.

"My planet is called Kleaditon!" she screamed, too, more from irritation at Jay's impatience than surprise.

"You are from another planet?"

Suddenly, the classroom door opened, and Jay snapped out. In an instant, his vision cleared up, and he was thrown from the cloud of Yelga's voice back to reality.

Cloe was standing by the door, smiling at him. She had put her hair up, and her collarbones were shining in tan golden.

"Who were you talking to?" she asked.

"No one," Jay said hastily and walked to his desk. "What do you want, Cloe? I haven't graded your last paper yet..."

"That's not why I'm here," Cloe interrupted him and closed the door.

Jay's eyes snapped to her catwalk and seductive eyes, lollipop still stuck between her lips.

"Please, open the door," he said strictly. "And leave it open."

"But Mr. Miller..." Cloe's doe-eyes rounded innocently as she drew closer and put her hand on his shoulder. "I want to be alone with you."

"Get away from me," startled, Jay stepped back. "You are a child, Cloe! And I'm your teacher. Your behavior is inappropriate."

"But would a child have body like this?" Cloe smirked and began to lift her shirt. "Oh, come on, Mr. Miller, I know you want it. I like you very much."

Before she could say more, Jay stepped back and dashed to the door. Feeling trapped like a mouse, he swung the door open and hurried out, his cheeks burning up.

Squeezed between the noisy crowds of students, he could feel his head spinning, every voice mixing and turning into an agony. He couldn't believe what Cloe had done and that he had let it happen - however short it was, it was still something.

It's my fault! I should have never smiled at her!

The image of Cloe's smirk and hands seductively rolling her shirt up twinkled in his eyes like burning pictures. Someone bumped into him, someone jolted his back, but he didn't care. All he wanted was to get away from her as soon and as far as possible.

Finally, when he came to his senses, Jay found himself in front of a school cafeteria.

Gasping for air, he stood crazed, looking into the room he knew well. The cafeteria had already been emptied of students who had grabbed their lunches and scattered around, and only a few people lingered by the tables. Empty packages and dirty plates were strewn around the room, the scent of cheap and fast food turning the air stuffy.

Remembering that he had to drink water and eat something to keep himself awake and sane, Jay walked to the buffet and bought some lunch: some salad and fries that he didn't even look at properly. Then, with hurried steps, he walked to a window seat and began eating quietly and alone.

The images of Cloe blended with the memory of the stranger's voice. What a weird day it was! So out of ordinary, but in a bad way. Jay felt his insides churning, his heart still galloping like a wild horse. He was chewing but couldn't taste the food, feeling as if he swallowed plastic. If only he could just go home and forget all about it.

When a chair was dragged out at his table, he lifted his head and gaped in horror, scared Cloe had found him. But relief washed over when he saw Kalpana, his colleague, a math teacher.

"Hi, Jay," she smiled. "Can I sit here?"

"Of course," Jay smiled back. This time, his smile was honest. He liked Kalpana, this sweet and kind lady who had welcomed him on the first day of his work. Since then, she has done nothing but make him comfortable, help him get to know the school and students, and answer any of his questions. Now, seeing her even soothed his heavy heart.

"Thank you," she said and took a seat slowly, carefully.

Jay diverted his eyes, scared he'd make her uncomfortable. An army veteran, Kalpana had a prosthetic leg, and though it could hardly be noticed in her slight limp, she never hid the truth from anyone. Jay respected her courage and confidence but could never manage to think of the right questions. So he just kept quiet.

"It's a beautiful day, isn't it?" Kalpana beamed and began sipping her orange juice.

She turned her head toward the window, and the sunshine, bursting through it, glinted off her glasses and reflected into her hazel-green eyes. The golden light poured into her honey-blonde hair and turned her pale skin milky-white and almost shimmery. Her smile was humble, almost shy but also self-assured, her plump lips lifting up genuinely, her eyes holding nothing but pure thoughts.

For a moment, Jay forgot all about the stranger's voice and sunk into the image of Kalpana. He had never truly seen her as a woman but only his friend and a colleague. But now, for the first time, he realized how attractive she was, how much warmth and light she radiated, how womanly and almost motherly she was. And despite things some would consider turning off: amputated leg, chubbier body shape, or nerdy glasses, she was pretty.

"I can hardly take my 8 graders anymore," Kalpana laughed and took a bite of her sandwich. She chewed slowly, covering her mouth with a hand. This feminine motion fits her character. "They have become unsocial, know it all! They don't even talk to each other but text all the time. And their grades are getting worse."

"Tell me about it," Jay laughed, nodding. "They don't even listen to me. Those who used to listen are turning into zombies, too."

"Yeah, yesterday one of my students...." Kalpana began, but Jay couldn't concentrate anymore.

As Kalpana's voice turned distant and hushed, as if she was talking from the bottom of an ocean, Jay's mind began flying back to Yelga and the strange things she had said to him. Kleanio, Dastario country, planet Kleaditon. How could he have never heard of these places? He had been learning about the Earth and every single city, town, or village it contained his whole life! Was it possible that a new country had been created, and he hadn't read the news about it? But how could this information slip by without his attention? But again, he could make some kind of sense of an unfamiliar country and town, but a planet? especially a planet with life on it? This sounded like a delusion, like some fairy tale that parents read to children before bed. This couldn't be real, no, no...

"Jay?"

Kalpana's voice dragged him out of the train of thought, and he saw her gaping at him worriedly. With her thin brows brought together, she watched him with concern as if he had just fallen sick.

"Are you okay?"

"Yeah, yeah," Jay shook his head and smiled at her. "Just overthinking, sorry."

"It's fine," Kalpana smiled back, her teeth shining like a set of pearls. "I get lost in my thoughts often, too."

He appreciated her understanding, nonjudgmental look. He almost thanked her, but in the end, he only smiled and got up.

"Have to go to the library for some research," he said, throwing the leftover food in a trash bin, almost filled to the rim. "See you later, Kalpana."

"Bye, Jay," she gave a little wave, dainty golden bracelet twinkling on her wrist.

With his head spinning from the unanswered questions that only kept growing, multiplying, and cramming his mind, Jay turned and headed toward the library. There, he could use any source available: computers or old books and newspapers to search for this strange planet. Only after he'd find proof of its existence would he believe that the woman in his head wasn't a product of his imagination.

Kalpana watched Jay as he walked away, her eyes fixed on his shoulders, aware that Jay was oblivious of her look. Now, when he couldn't see her, she could watch him as much as she wanted, she could smile at herself and imagine for a moment that they were a couple.

Her heart was aching, almost to the point of bursting, but not from pain. She had gotten used to the fact that they would never be together. How could Jay accept love from a handicapped woman five years older than him? She could only daydream and cherish the moments she spent with him, even if they were only friendly.

He was definitely thinking of someone else, Kalpana was sure of it. Only a love interest can distract you as much as Jay was distracted during lunch.

Sighing, Kalpana turned her head back to the window and closed her eyes under the warm rays of sunshine. She was grateful she got to be around Jay, even if it was only for a short while. If she saw him just a couple of times a week, she didn't need anything else.

The library was quiet and peaceful. Relieved that he could calmly drown in his thoughts without anyone disturbing him, Jay walked into the narrow aisles of the bookcases.

The library was the only room he liked in the school. The windows were wide and let the light drench the walls. The furniture: long tables, comfortable armchairs, and tall and heavy bookcases were made of wood, vintage and well-kept, and the woody smell turned the atmosphere cozy and relaxed. He loved the scent of old books and yellowing paper, the coffee that the librarian made for herself, and the silence that could never exist outside of this room. He loved taking his time when he was working or reading here. He would always choose the coziest corner, sink into a leather chair with a lamp by his side, and spend hours before the librarian reminded him that she had to close it up.

But now, he didn't have time to spare, so he walked with haste. The beams of sunlight sifted into the passages walled by books like into tall forest trees. Jay, passing the students quietly reading or doing their homework - a rare kind in the school - headed toward the computer section. There, five computers were lined up on separate desks, and he took a seat by one, quickly typing in the names he'd been wondering about.

His fingers moved like spider legs on the keyboard, and his clicking on a computer mouse filled his surroundings. But the Internet showed him nothing, correcting Kleanio into Kleanco, turning Dastario into disastrous, and writing Kleidion instead of Kleaditon.

Finally, Jay gave up. Exhaling a deep sigh, he turned the computer off and rubbed his eyes. He felt them stinging, but that didn't quell his curiosity. He couldn't help but keep searching.

The thick-covered books called out to him from the back of the library. Leaving the overheated computer, he headed toward the area he knew the best and visited the most often: the geography section.

It was completely empty, as mostly it was, and Jay stood in front of the stacked shelves, his eyes roaming over the books and their titles. He had read most of it but only a few that were too old, published in the late 50ies and 60ies. Thinking that because he couldn't find anything in the information the modern world provided, he could find something in vintage publications.

He gently slid his fingertips over the books, leaving traces on their dusty surface. Then he dragged them out, heavy and huge, with dark covers and big, bold titles, and began sifting through them. He stopped at every word resembling those he was looking for, reading quickly but attentively, using all his skills of information searching.

But when his eyes began to sting too much, he realized that he was reading in gloom. He lifted his head, ache running from his neck to his back, his shoulders cracking. When he looked around the half-empty library, he realized hours had passed without him even noticing.

The evening had descended. Surrounded by books, Jay realized that all his attempts were futile. He couldn't fine the country or planet in any text and he had wasted whole day on it!

Putting everything back on the shelves, he dragged himself up from the floor.

The lamps had turned on, brightening up the room in dim yellow. Sun had set behind the horizon and dark blue sipped into the sky. Now it was quiet outside too, empty of the students and teachers.

Jay looked back, realizing there was only him and the librarian left, as often happened. She saw him too and smiled, her wrinkly face turning more wrinkled.

"Hi, Magda," he smiled as he walked to her desk.

She pushed her oval glasses up on his nose and opened thin, shriveled lips.

"Good evening, Jay," she said. "Getting lost in books again, are you?"

"Yeah," he laughed. "But I need your help today."

She raised her nonexistent brows and tugged on a lacy collar of her white shirt that she must have had since the 80ies.

"I need newspapers," he said. "Anything important, especially containing information about planets."

Magda frowned, pondering.

"We don't have many newspapers here," she said. "But there's some in the archive. You need it today?"

"Yes, please, if it's possible," Jay put on the most charming smile he could.

It took half an hour for Magda to gather everything she considered helpful and bring it to Jay, who waited with a cup of coffee and a heavy head. After thanking her and promising to bring everything safe and intact, Jay grabbed his bag and hurried home, impatient to find something in the newspapers - his last hope.

CHAPTER 2
Unexpected Friendship

An annoying, shrill sound of the alarm clock woke Jay up, the sunshine burning the side of his face while the other stuck to his pillow.

Disoriented, he lifted his head and rubbed his eyes. The sight of the newspapers scattered all around him - on the bed and floor - made him remember how he had spent the night: reading every article possible until he fell asleep fully clothed, with the lamp on, at 4 in the morning.

"God," he grunted and sat up on his elbows.

The morning brought light onto his messy bedroom, clothes spread around, paper boxes of takeout strewed, books open and abandoned in the corner, ungraded paper, and unfinished work left ignored on a desk.

"I need to tidy up this place," he murmured and got up, carefully gathering the newspapers, hoping Magda wouldn't notice the few wrinkled edges.

But nothing discouraged him more - not even the fact that he hadn't checked his students' assignments and homework - than the fact that he hadn't found anything about Kleanio, Dastario, or Kleaditon. He stopped, trying to listen to his mind. But the voice was gone, and his head was quiet.

"Perhaps it was just all imaginary," he murmured as he headed to a bathroom. "I was too exhausted yesterday." Looking into the mirror, Jay laughed sarcastically. "I can't believe I thought it was real! And I was even looking for it! How foolish."

After half an hour of morning routine, he was ready, looking fresh in white shirt and dress pants, his satchel over his shoulder, hair tucked behind his ears. He needed to book a haircut but he didn't know when he would have time for that. For now, clean clothes would have to do.

It was a beautiful day, but Jay couldn't notice. Hurrying, he got in his car and turned the keys. It didn't take long before he got stuck in traffic and nervous he'd be late for his first class; he began tapping on the steering wheel.

The more he thought about how much time he had spent searching for the nonexistent planet, the more his anger rolled up and turned bigger, crawling up to his throat. He felt stupid and insane, irritated at his nativity. His mind had played tricks on him, and he grabbed the bait like the stupidest fish.

The traffic light shone red, and he stopped, his car engine vibrating under him. The streets were crammed and noisy, with blaring, honking, and beeping, but at least he was close to school.

His eyes jumped nervously to the red light when suddenly he fell into the familiar trance: surroundings blurred, noises hushed. And he realized the voice was back.

"Hey, Jay!" Yelga's voice appeared. "How are you?"

"It's you again?!" Jay almost yelled from shock. "Aren't you imagination?"

"No!" Yelga laughed. "I thought *you* were my imagination. But I think we are both real."

A pause fell as they both waited for each other to speak.

"I couldn't stop thinking about you," Yelga spoke. "And I tried to find things out about your planet Earth but couldn't. I don't think my people know about it."

"And I couldn't find anything about *your* planet."

Yelga's voice was soothing and gentle; her words formed delicately and with thought.

"Your place, your country, you. all of this seems..." Yelga seemed to smile. "I dont know, I have no answers. I thought I was going crazy but... can you tell me how we are talking to each other now?"

"I don't know," Jay felt his nervousness dying down. "You're in my mind."

"Yes! I just talked to you, and you answered," Yelga laughed, her laugh vibrating through his ears like silver bells. "Are you real?"

"I am very real," now Jay couldn't help but laugh too. "Are you?"

"Of course I am!"

"Then the only explanation I can find is that..." Jay swallowed. "We are from two different planets, different universes even."

"That's what I think too!" Yelga's voice turned excited. "somehow, by some cosmic connection we telepath from different solar systems. Don't ask me how, I don't know yet but what I know is that we hear each other and we understand each other."

Understand, that was a nice word for this situation. Jay smiled.

"Well, then, tell me more about you," he said. "Maybe over time, we can figure out this mystery."

Those five remaining minutes of drive to work felt like hours as Jay conversed with Yelga, and by the time he reached the school parking, he felt as if he knew a lot about her, but not too much - just enough not to consider her a stranger anymore, but also leaving Jay intrigued, curious to find out more and continue their conversation. As if he had been on a first date, which had gone better than expected, and he couldn't wait for their second date. He had bonded with Yelga effortlessly, their dialogue building without any force, their thought exchange natural and comforting. It was one of those rare situations when he didn't even need to try to connect with the woman, and it happened without him even noticing; when he didn't feel even a bit of stress and instead relaxed, opened himself up completely and didn't hold his true self back. Yelga's voice raised immediate trust in him, her comments and reactions funny and empathetic, so smart and logical that it was clear she listened closely, sipped up his every word. In return, she showed Jay her real self, shared her story, and let him peek into her world.

As he turned the car keys off and put her hands away from the wheel, Jay realized he was still smiling, his face hurting from it. This unusual high that talking with Yelga had brought him, this euphoria that he was completely immersed in, was making him feel younger, lighter, excited, and restless but relaxed and calm at the same time - as if he was a teenage boy, kissing a girl for the first time. But this ecstasy was even more magical as it was emptied of everything physical, free of everything material. Only two celestial beings connecting.

With a jolt, he realized that he had to start his day. However much he wanted to spend every minute talking to Yelga, he had real life to go back to.

"Sorry, my class is starting," he said, hoping Yelga wouldn't hear the despair in his voice.

"No worries. I have to go back to work too, finish my painting," Yelga said unhurriedly.

She was a painter and a true artist, and that threw Jay into another whirlwind of affection.

"I've always wanted to be an artist but never had any talent," he laughed. "All I can do is appreciate it from afar."

"I'm sure you are talented in a way you don't know yet," Yelga responded. "My mother made her first sculpture when she was 47. Now she's one of the most famous artists in our country."

"Well, then, I have 19 years left to figure out what my talent is."

They both laughed.

"Okay, bye for now, Jay," Yelga said and her voice growing faint like a vivid colored paint fading into a river.

"Bye, Yelga."

Back in the real, less colorful, and exciting world, Jay worked his way through the aisles of cars - giant metal bugs - and headed into the school.

Walking among the noisy, blaring crowds of students, passing by his colleagues with formal greetings, and preparing himself for his first class, Jay couldn't help but think of Yelga again and again. Memories of her voice came back to him every other minute, making him smile to himself.

Only when he reached his classroom and ran his eyes over the kids filling rows of desks, he realized that his morning irritation had disappeared and he didn't dread his work day as much anymore. In fact, he was looking forward to it because at the end, the possibility of talking to Yelga was waiting.

So, with a bright smile and hearty greeting, he stepped into the room.

The days began to start and end with Yelga. Waking up, Jay heard her silvery voice and sprung from his bed instead of sleeping in or groaning out of it as he used to do. His morning routines were accompanied by Yelga's funny stories, thoughtful suggestions or smart insights about some topics. Though their worlds were different - even universes were different! - they seemed to share a lot and have more in common than expected. He shared the knowledge about Earth with her and she told him about Kleaditon.

"It's completely blue?!" Jay couldn't hold back his surprise. "There is no other color?"

"No! We have dozens of shades of blue," Yelga laughed at his surprise. "What other colors are there to exist?"

"So many! You don't even know!" Jay said and was about to continue when he realized how hard and almost impossible it was to describe a color.

"We have a color yellow, which is a color of light, a color of warm sand, and a friend's kind smile," he said. "Red, which is a color of passion! The color of rage and beautiful women. And we have white. It's a symbol of purity, peace, and calm. It's a color of innocence and... your voice."

He heard Yelga smile.

"And we have so many other colors," he continued, and now Yelga couldn't hide her shock.

Their surprises were endless as days went on, and their conversations grew longer and deeper. It was nighttime for Yelga when Jay was getting ready for work, and sometimes, she disappeared for hours when she had to paint. But Jay waited patiently, even the thought of talking to her making him beam.

Yelga's voice followed Jay like a soothing background music. On the way to work, during breaks, heading home, staying in on the evening - he spent it all conversing with her and he never got bored of it.

Their talking subjects included everything from their childhood to their goals, world problems, deep fears, family relationships, and pet peeves. But one thing Jay could never get himself to ask was what grew his curiosity more and more: what did Yelga look like? He knew he couldn't ask, it would be rude and materialistic and he was afraid of discouraging Yelga.

So, all he could do was imagine. At first, he imagined a normal woman, a human woman. Tall, lean, with long dark hair and deep, sensitive eyes. He imagined her sitting by her kitchen table, eating breakfast while they chatted, cleaning her house, putting on an apron before grabbing paint brushes and perching in front of a huge canvas.

But then, his images slowly shifted like Polaroid pictures blurring in water. The more he learned about Kleaditon, the more he understood that Yelga wasn't a normal person. It was hard to see her as someone else - or something else. Squeezing his eyes shut, Jay tried to imagine an alien, the tall and oval-headed creature that humankind means when they say 'alien.' But perhaps Yelga was different; perhaps she was completely different, truly magical and beautiful, with sparkling diamond skin and big space-blue eyes. Maybe she was not even close to what Jay imagined. Maybe she didn't even have a physical form. He didn't know, and he realized he had no desire to find out. Yelga's voice was enough for her existence, and Jay didn't want to ask for more.

CHAPTER 3
New Life

The warm afternoon promised a cool and peaceful night. The music was on a low volume, chatter soft and almost comforting, the breeze slipping through tree branches and bringing the tasty scent of sausages roasting on a grill.

Standing with a bottle of beer in his hand, Jay felt at ease, smiling while half-listening to his colleagues. Smith, the literature teacher, had invited the teachers to a barbeque party on a sunny Saturday, and for the first time, Jay had accepted the invite. And now, he was glad that he had.

It could hardly be called a party. It was just a gathering of middle-aged teachers, a chance to relax outside of school, drink and eat, and talk their hearts out about their unruly students. Jay was the youngest one there, and he had never thought he could have anything in common with his colleagues: they were mostly divorced and boring people with no goals or aims, used to their ordinary lives. But it turned out he had quite a lot to talk to them about, and he thought that maybe their ordinary lives weren't that bad.

The sun was about to set, burnt orange rays sifting through the leaves. The food was delicious and though the beer was cheap, it went well with the barbeque atmosphere. Biting into a hot dog, Jay walked away from the chatter group, slowly striding on the freshly mowned loan, passing Smith's one-floor, modest but well-kept, white house and looking at the sunset.

His mind wondered off to his morning conversation with Yelga. They had talked about their future and he couldn't throw her words out of his head: I want healthy children and a happy marriage, everything else can be fixed or overcome.

"Turns out we aren't that bad, right?" he heard and looked back.

Kalpana was smiling at him. Her gaze was as kind and attentive as usual, her voice careful. She had put her hair up and looked younger. With slow steps and a slight limp, she walked up to him.

"Yeah, I'm glad I came," Jay smiled.

"I'm glad you did, too. You never did before."

"That's my loss," he said apologetically.

Kalpana laughed, and they stood side by side, watching the sun slide behind the distant mountains and coloring them in reddish pink. They were quiet for a while, and the ambiance felt benign.

"You seem happy lately," suddenly Kalpana said. Her cheeks flushed when Jay turned his head at her. "I mean happier."

He laughed. "No, you're right. I was miserable before. But..." he paused, smiling. "Yeah, I feel better."

"Did something good happen?"

Jay shrugged. He couldn't tell his secret, the biggest secret that he could never speak of.

"Nothing in particular. I guess I changed my perspective." He said. "I try to make the most out of it, you know? Try to enjoy classes, and that helps me realize that it's not that boring."

"That's nice," Kalpana laughed, then her face shifted into a gentle smile. "I'm glad you feel that way."

He peeled his eyes off the sun and looked at her. She had never stood so close before, and now, Jay could see the brownish dots in her green eyes. Light freckles followed her cheeks and nose bridge, and she radiated a sweet scent of vanilla.

She was smiling up at him, with her eyes sparkling but asking for nothing - as if she just wanted to stand there and watch him. Her attention washed over Jay, shaking him with realization - who else in his life could notice a change in him? Who else was glad that he seemed happy?

Kalpana was right there, smiling at him, and he felt the words gathering at his lips, the only words that seemed right at that moment.

"Would you like to have dinner with me sometimes?"

Startled, Kalpana widened her eyes, her face warping with surprise and then reddening up from delight. Her unhidden joy revealed how long she'd been waiting to hear these words.

"Yes!" she nodded.

Jay smiled, feeling content. It was a rare and new feeling, and he knew he had done the right thing. Why did he have to deny himself love if it was right there in front of him? Yelga was the woman he would have spent his whole life with. But she wasn't there; she wasn't his future. And Kalpana was standing beside him, ready to offer him the world.

The early Autumn night brought a chilly breeze, clouds casting the sky and lowering to the ground, heavy with raindrops. Streetlights glinted in yellow along the roads like flickering fireflies, houses brightened by the artificial light coming from their windows. Dark silhouettes of families mingled behind them, gathering at the end of the day, ready to relax before TV and in the company of their loved ones.

It was a peaceful autumn night, and Jay was lying in his bed, tired after the long work day. He had returned a few hours ago, and as soon as he slipped out of his work clothes, he flopped on the bed and began talking to Yelga. With his hands folded under his head, he was staring up at the ceiling with a smile as if he were watching a movie. But in reality, he was watching nothing - he saw or heard nothing but Yelga's voice that came like rippling waves, making him lose the sense of time and place. In moments like this - when he was alone and could unhurriedly chat with her - Jay felt the most at ease, the most delighted. Nothing relaxed him more after a stressful and exhausting day of having five classes and grading assignments for hours - not even a hot bath, not even a few glasses of cold red wine, not even watching trash TV with a bowl of popcorn. Yelga was what he wanted, all the time, without any replacement.

"I would love to see your paintings," Jay said, his feet dancing at the edge of the bed, unknown to him.

"I would love to show you," Yelga responded. She sounded as calm as always but there was something else in her voice too - gentleness, newfound fondness that only very close people let each other feel. "But I don't think that's possible."

"Maybe we can make it happen," Jay said, trying to sound hopeful. The thought of never meeting Yelga was one of his deepest fears. "Miracles happen."

Jay sighed and rolled to his side, grabbing a book he had been reading in his spare time, which was less now as he filled most of it with Yelga.

"I've been reading a book about three colors. They are essays about blue, yellow, and red. I wanted to read you something." he said and flipped the book to the part he had saved. He felt Yelga's attention pricking up, ready to hear something beautiful, and he didn't want to disappoint. "There's this passage that made me think of you."

He cleared his throat, sitting up to see the page under his dim lamp light.

"Blue is a mysterious color," he began with a smile. "Hue of illness and nobility, the rarest color in nature. It is the color of ambiguous depth, of the heavens and of the abyss at once; blue is the color of the shadow side, the tint of the marvelous and the inexplicable, and of desire…"

He stopped, waiting to hear Yelga's reaction. As he listened to the silence, the book still open in his hands, he heard something beating and realized it was his heart - racing, trying to jump out of his chest like a bird crushing against walls of a cage. He was nervous! For the first time in a while, he was nervous like a little boy and he didn't know why.

"Every time I see blue, I think of you," he said in a quiet voice, almost murmuring it. "Which is many times a day."

"That's a beautiful passage, Jay," Yelga finally responded. "And I always think of you too. Even though I can't see you, you are an inseparable part of my life."

Silence fell between them again - stretching over the distance of a million light years - and Jay heard his heartbeat again. That's all he could hear, and he wondered what Yelga's heartbeat sounded like.

He waited, and he knew she was waiting, too. They were waiting for each other to say those words - those three words that hung on the tip of Jay's tongue.

A sudden ring of the doorbell jolted Jay, and he snapped out. Realizing Kalpana had come, he sat up on the bed.

"Sorry, I have to go," he said. "Talk to you at our usual time?"

Seemingly still drawing in the confused silence, Yelga took a few seconds to answer.

"Yes," she said. "Our usual time tomorrow."

They had created a schedule for their conversations as both wanted this unusual relationship not to ruin their real ones but, at the same time, to continue talking. They had forbidden talking at work or when they were around other people, putting a time limit to their dialogues - mostly at night or in the early morning and twice a day on weekends.

Stepping into his slippers, Jay scurried to the door and opened it up.

Kalpana stood with a bright smile and grocery bags in her hands. She stepped in and leaned to Jay, giving him a soft and long kiss before she passed by him and headed to his kitchen.

"I brought ingredients for pesto pasta!" she said aloud, opening Jay's fridge. I hope you're hungry!"

Still shaken, Jay slowly closed the door.

"Yeah!" he responded distractedly. "I am."

He couldn't forget the tense silence between him and Yelga, those expectant moments that could have ended in a way he dreamed of.

Bowls and pans rattled in the kitchen, and Jay looked through the doorway to see Kalpana get ready to prepare dinner. With her hair in a bun, she wore an apron and was washing tomatoes. Smiley and energetic, she looked comfortable in Jay's kitchen, familiar with the surroundings and aware of every object and their places.

It had been over three months since they had started officially dating, and though they hadn't moved in together, they were now visiting and staying over at one another's place as often as they wanted. All the initial awkwardness was erased, and they were now completely used to each other's presence, habits and adapting to their different lifestyles. Jay liked Kalpana more and more, he liked her enthusiasm and readiness to please him. Cooking was her love language, and she showed it often, making food for Jay, which was so good he had suggested Kalpana learn cooking professionally. On this, Kalpana had laughed, kissed Jay, and said that no one liked her food as much as him.

"How was your day?" she asked when Jay walked into the kitchen and began boiling pasta.

"Fine," he smiled.

"Did the presentation go well?"

She always remembered what Jay told her, important or unimportant things and that was one of the traits Jay loved the most about her.

"Yeah, the school director actually liked it very much. He might promote me from a teacher to a counselor."

"That's amazing! Congratulations!" Kalpana exclaimed.

"Well, nothing's definite yet," he said humbly.

"I'm sure you'll get it," she kissed him gently, her eyes genuine and loving.

The dinner passed by in peace, accompanied by soft and classical music Kalapana put on her phone, delicious food that made the whole house smell like a restaurant, and conversation about trivial things. In the end, they washed the dishes, Kalpana soaping, and Jay rinsing them like a long-time married couple.

Then, watching a movie, they sprawled on the sofa, Kalpana's head on his shoulder, his hand over hers. It was one of those cozy nights-in that Jay loved. He loved feeling Kalpana's vanilla scent, sitting with her body clinging against his, watching a dumb rom-com that made them laugh, drinking wine, and chatting about anything that came to their minds.

"Thank you for the dinner; it was amazing," Jay looked at her when they turned the movie on.

The TV light brightened their faces, the characters' dramatic voices faded in the background, their vivid silhouettes quickly replaced each other on the screen.

"You're welcome," she said. "I love you."

"I love you too," he said, kissing his girlfriend, feeling the taste of her strawberry lip-gloss.

He said it, and he meant it; he always did. But now, something churned deep in his heart, a quiet voice whispering in his ear that he wasn't honest. He loved Kalpana, but she wasn't the only woman he loved.

When Kalapna slid closer to him and put her head on his shoulder, looking back at the screen, Jay couldn't help but wonder what Yelga's lips tasted like.

CHAPTER 4
Broken Hearts

Holding hands, Jay and Kalpana strolled through a park, enjoying the sunny spring day. Flowers had started to bloom, their colors bright and eye-catching. The tree branches were rising to the blue sky, heavy with myriads of leaves. Narrow paths snaked among trimmed grass and wildflowers, pine trees, and stone sculptures. Many couples had come outside, strolling like Jay and Kalpana, in comfortable silence, gazing at the scenery while also enjoying each other's company.

"I'm so glad spring is finally here," Kalpana said as they passed a sculpture of a deer and saw two birds sitting on its antlers, chirping. "March was horrible."

"Yeah, it was basically winter, worse than February," Jay laughed.

Cats were rolled up on a fence, bathing in the light. The world was waking up from the winter slumber, coming out to bask in the sun.

"I love taking walks with you. This park is beautiful," he said, and he squeezed Kalpana's hand tighter.

With the corner of his eye, Jay felt Kalpana staring at him intensely as if trying to lazer through his face with his eyes.

He turned his head, looking at her. Kalpana's eyes were sparkling, her whole face shiny as if she had swallowed all the sunlight.

Suddenly, she stopped and holding her hand, Jay had to stop, too.

"I want to ask you something," Kalpana started slowly, taking a long pause. Then she gazed up into his eyes, happy but nervous. "Will you marry me?"

It caught Jay by surprise. They had been dating for a while and fell more and more in love, but he didn't expect or plan a marriage anytime soon.

But Kalpana spread her happiness onto him, too, and standing in the company of blooming flowers and rising sun, Jay found no reason to say no. At that moment, he would say everything Kalpana asked for.

"Yes, I will marry you," Jay laughed. "Let's get married."

With a joyful shriek, Kalpana wrapped her arms around his neck and kissed him. Only hours later, when they returned home, and the gloom began to fall, Jay felt the realization heavy in his heart - he had to talk to Yelga.

It took him a few days to summon the courage, and finally, one evening, he felt like it was the right time to say it - he couldn't stretch it out anymore.

"Yelga, I have something to tell you," he swallowed. He was standing by his window, alone in a dark room. "I love you."

Yelga fell quiet, and Jay felt that surprise had turned her speechless.

"I love you too," Yelga said in a few seconds. "I've loved you for a while, Jay."

"I'm so happy to hear you say that," Jay couldn't conceal his delight. His smile slowly melted. "But I have something to tell you. I know I should have told you sooner, but I was scared of losing you."

"What is it?" Yelga's voice turned concerned.

"I've been dating a woman, and... she asked me to marry her. I said yes."

He continued speaking, telling Yelga everything about his relationship with Kalpana, revealing all he had been hiding before.

"I'm sorry; I shouldn't have kept this from you," he could feel tears rising in his eyes. "Please, don't hate me."

"So, you're in love with someone else too," Yelga said. For the first time, her voice was angry and disappointed, piercing through Jay's heart like sharp blades. "How could you hide this from me for so long?"

Jay listened quietly, out of words. He knew he was at fault and couldn't defend himself.

"I thought we shared everything with each other," Yelga added.

"You're right," Jay responded. "But Kalpana was so kind to me; I wanted to share my earthly life with her. I just couldn't help myself, I was lonely. If you were here, everything would be different, but... we are so far away."

Yelga was quiet for a while, thinking about his words.

"I understand," she said, startling Jay. "You have your own life, and I have mine."

Her empathy was bigger than Jay had known and now his heart swelled with gratitude, his tears releasing the tension. He was relieved.

"I met someone too, but I didn't let myself feel anything for them because of you, because I love you," she said. "But I know it's time I move on from the fantasy that we will meet someday. I feel it's right to let myself live, love someone, and build a family, just like you."

"We will always be friends," Jay smiled. "We'll always be in each other's minds."

"You'll always be my biggest and strangest love," Yelga smiled too.

They were quiet for a while, each to their thoughts. Jay's eyes lingered on a butterfly twirling around a dandelion in his garden.

"You will have to tell her too, Jay," Yelga spoke.

"I know," Jay sighed. He dreaded revealing his secret to Kalpana, still searching for words that wouldn't make him sound like an insane person and a deceitful boyfriend.

It was a rainy evening when Jay confessed to Kalpana. She was repotting her plants, and Jay helped. He watched how carefully Kalpana held the peace lily not to harm the pearl white flower that had just sprouted, how delicately she handled lilac orchids, and how slowly she slid African violets into new pots she had painted in different colors and patterns. Only after dating her did Jay learn how crafty and artsy Kalpana was, the math teacher that he could never imagine was crocheting, sculpting clay, and growing plants in her free time. The closer they got, the more Jay discovered about her and saw how big Kalpana's world was, how colorful and fulfilling. He joked that she never got bored because she always had something to busy herself with. And he tried to pick up some of her hobbies. She was the most grounded person he knew.

"I have a secret," he said suddenly. "And I've had it quite a while."

Kalpana, holding Spider plant in her hands, stopped, turning her head to him.

"What secret?" her voice dripped with fear.

"Um..." Jay took a deep breath and took his gloves off. So did Kalpana, putting them away and they flopped on the floor, surrounded by unrooted plants and soil scattered around.

"I've been talking to someone. We started before you and I began dating," Jay said, dropping his head, unable to look into her eyes, her big, deep eyes that were now walled with anxiety and apprehension.

Rain pattered against the windows like a little girl tapping her fingertips on the glass while Jay spoke about his and Yelga's story. His eyes were fixed on the floor as he talked for a while, telling Kalpana everything that she deserved to know. The rain got heavier, rattling on the roof and breaking the tense silence that fell whenever Jay took a pause, but it still wasn't loud enough to overpower the sound of his racing heart.

Finally, when he looked up, his chest tightened. Kalpana was watching him with teary eyes, her face contorted with utter sadness.

He apologized, asked for forgiveness, and repeated on and on that he loved her, but Kalpana didn't say a word.

Wiping her eyes, she stood up, turning her back to Jay to hide her face.

"You loved her even before you met me," she said finally.

"But it doesn't mean I love you any less," Jay pleaded.

"And you kept talking to her. This is emotional cheating." She turned, her cheeks red and wet. "I have to think about it... I need to be alone for a while."

Jay nodded and got up. "I'll give you space, but please, don't forget what we have. It is special."

He left and waited to hear from Kalpana but the more he did, the less hopeful he felt. Desperate, he kept blaming himself for messing the best thing up in his life. It was only his fault, no one else's.

However, on the 8th day, Kalpana knocked on his door, and after a moment of silence at his doorstep, they fell into each other's arms.

"You really hurt me, Jay," she sobbed in his embrace. "But I love you so much."

"I promise I will never hide anything from you ever again," he said.

And he kept his promise. During their thirty-five years of marriage, through all the hardships and happiness they endured, through raising three kids, moving four times, retiring, and saying goodbye to their adult children - Jay never lied to Kalpana, never kept secrets from her, and never broke her heart again.

It's Not The End

Jay stood by a window while a warm evening coated the village with dark blue paint that dribbled over tall, snow-covered mountains and into the woods. The trees wavered through the soft breeze, the last strings of rosy sunset filtering through the branches and glossy leaves. Only beetles crawled through the satiny grass while everything else fell into quiet. The silence poured out of the forest, leading to the dark, and the two spread around Jay's house like two best friends holding hands.

"Oh, I love this place so much," he said. "Moving here is one of the best decisions Kalpana and I have ever made."

"It must be nice," Yelga responded. "To live peacefully, especially now that we are so old."

"We aren't that old!" Jay laughed.

Smiling, Jay nodded and put candles on. They glinted in soothing yellow, breaking the gloom.

"Okay, maybe not that old," Yelga chuckled. Her laughs sounded the same as thirty-five years ago, silver bells ringing. "But in the age where we need peace and beautiful scenery."

"Well, that is true."

Jay looked down on his wrinkled hands, listening to crickets chirping outside.

"How are you doing?" he asked softly. "I know it's still hard."

"Yes, it is," Yelga answered, her voice melancholic. "It's been only two months, and I'm still grieving, but I'm getting better. I know that's what my husband would want me to do."

Jay nodded. He wanted to hug her and console her, but he could only share his feelings.

"How are kids doing?" Yelga asked.

"Oh, the little one just turned 3, we threw him a birthday party last week," Jay's eyes lit up. "I can't believe I'm a grandfather of five!"

"That must feel amazing, right?" Yelga giggled. "And I remember you once saying you didn't want kids."

"I was a different man back then," Jay guffawed, shaking his head with embarrassment.

The tea kettle whistled, and Jay put it aside. He poured the boiling tea into a mug, the tangy aroma of lemon and orange spreading between the wooden walls.

His eyes peered toward the newspaper sitting on his kitchen counter. He grabbed it, looking at the first page with a humorous beam.

"They're still writing about us," he said, reading. "Still calling it breaking news even though the first article was published two weeks ago!"

"Still trending topic in scientific society?" Yelga seemed to smile gently.

"Yes!" Jay's eyes ran over the printed text. "Cosmic anomaly that connects two people from two planets of two different universes... Are people on Kleaditon still talking about it, too?"

"They are, and they are even more curious now. I'm a little tired of their questions, to be honest."

They laughed.

"Still can't figure out how people found out," He said.

"Me neither. Our spouses were the only ones who knew, and they would never say a word to anyone."

Jay put the newspaper aside, sipping his tea. He was hungry but wanted to wait. Kalpana would soon be back from grocery shopping, and they would make dinner together.

"Lately, I catch myself getting excited for the most mundane things," he said. "Like making dinner with my wife, going for an afternoon walk, or sitting in my garden and reading. Is that boring?"

"No," Yelga's voice coated his heart like dribbling honey. "It means that you are happy."

Jay scoffed. "I guess you are right."

They enjoyed silence for a while, Jay gazing out at the mountains, imagining how Yelga watched the blue scenery of her town.

"What are your plans for tomorrow?" he asked and listened as Yelga began telling him all about the ordinary tasks and routines of her everyday life.

While the sun sunk behind the sparkling white tips of the mountains, the two friends talked, enjoying their conversation as if they were side by side and the distance of millions of light

years between them didn't exist.